THE TREASURE

DRA
GIRLS

Mei the Ruby Treasure Dragon

Maddy Mara

Published in the UK by Scholastic, 2023
1 London Bridge, London, SE1 9BG
Scholastic Ireland, 89E Lagan Road, Dublin Industrial Estate,
Glasnevin, Dublin, D11 HP5F

First published in the US by Scholastic Inc., 2021

ISBN 978 0702 33032 2

A CIP catalogue record for this book is available from the British Library.

Printed and bound in Great Britain by Clays Ltd, Elcograf S.p.A
Paper made from wood grown in sustainable forests and other
controlled sources.

1 3 5 7 9 10 8 6 4 2

Book design by Stephanie Yang

www.scholastic.co.uk

DRAGON GIRLS

Mei the Ruby Treasure Dragon

by Maddy Mara

On Wednesdays, Mei had jewellery-making class after school. It was her favourite time of the week. Mei loved bright, sparkly things, so making jewellery was a dream come true. She learned how to cut copper wire with one set of pliers. She twisted it into loops with another. She threaded beads in perfect colour combinations and gave her pretty creations to friends at school.

The class was held at the community centre on the edge of the forest. On the first day, Mei made friends with two other girls named Aisha and Quinn. The three girls were all very different from one another, but together they just clicked. The second time class met, the new friends made matching bracelets. Mei's featured a gorgeous ruby-coloured bead. Aisha's had a sapphire-blue bead and Quinn's was jade green. The beads were only made of glass, but that didn't matter. Mei, Aisha and Quinn had created the bracelets together, which made them worth more than diamonds.

They loved their jewellery teacher, Ms Ahmed. She had long, dark hair and wore rings on every finger. She always brought a thermos of hot chocolate for the students to share and played music so they could sing along as they worked. Mei and Aisha were OK singers, but Quinn's voice was amazing.

Snow fell outside as Mei worked on her latest

creation. She was making a necklace for her mum, but she still hadn't finished when it was time to pack up. Time went by so quickly in this class!

Aisha and Quinn waved goodbye and dashed off.

"Can I stay a few more minutes?" Mei begged Ms Ahmed. "It's Mum's birthday tomorrow and her necklace isn't ready yet."

"Sure. You keep working while I return the tools to the storage closet," Ms Ahmed said, picking up a box of pliers.

Happily, Mei bent over the necklace again. As she worked, she became aware of a soft voice singing:

Magic Forest, Magic Forest, come explore...

Mei glanced around the room. Ms Ahmed had left the music playing, but the singing wasn't coming from the speaker.

Mei looked out the window. Soft, sparkling snow carpeted the ground. The beautiful singing seemed to be coming from the nearby forest, but Mei couldn't spot anyone out there.

Magic Forest, Magic Forest, come explore...

The words seemed to get louder, and the red bead in Mei's friendship bracelet twinkled brightly. Mei wrapped her fingers around the ruby. Heat spread through her, like when she wrapped her hands around a warm mug on a cold day.

Releasing her fingers, Mei gazed at the bead. Deep within the glass, a shape formed. It was a little like the swirl in a marble. But this was different. This shape looked like a tree, no taller than a fingernail. The tree was graceful, lush and . . . *moving*. Yes, the tiny tree inside Mei's bead was swaying back and forth!

Was this a magical bead? Excitedly, Mei held her bracelet up to the light. As she watched, the red glow from the bead started to expand. It grew larger and larger, swelling like a balloon of light. The whispery song became clearer.

Magic Forest, Magic Forest, come explore.
Magic Forest, Magic Forest, hear my roar!

The tiny tree had grown with the red glow, and now there were other trees, too. Soon they were taller than Mei! Her heart thumped. She began to spin around and around. It made her dizzy, but she couldn't stop!

A warm breeze wrapped around Mei and lifted her off the ground. She found herself singing the words she'd heard, as though it was a song she'd always known:

Magic Forest, Magic Forest, come explore.

Magic Forest, Magic Forest, hear my roar!

Mei closed her eyes. All her life, she had longed to go on wild adventures. Now, finally, it felt like something truly magical was actually happening!

Mei landed back on the ground. She stopped spinning and opened her eyes. When the swirling red light cleared, Mei saw that she was no longer in the community centre. The tables and chairs, the big windows overlooking the forest, the containers of beads and wire and clasps – they had all disappeared!

Instead, Mei was in some sort of forest – and it was no longer winter. The snow had vanished, and she was surrounded by leafy trees. The air smelled of flowers and ripe tropical fruits. As Mei looked around in amazement, a bird flashed by. Its wings were green with yellow spots, tipped with pink.

Everything around her had changed. *Have I changed, too?* Mei wondered.

She felt different, somehow. Looking down, Mei gasped. Her black jeans and chunky boots were gone. Her legs had changed shape and were now covered in the brightest ruby-red scales. And instead of feet, she had powerful red paws!

Now Mei was dying of curiosity. She *had* to see what the rest of her body looked like. She glanced around. She didn't really expect to find a mirror in the middle of this forest – but then again, anything was possible in this strange place! Nearby, a shimmering lake surrounded by reeds glinted in the sunshine. Mei bounded over to it and peered into the smooth surface of the water.

Looking back at her was a ruby face with big dark eyes, an elegant snout, and twitching, pointed red ears.

"I'm a dragon?" Mei whispered to herself, laughing.

Mei loved acting and had played many different characters in school productions. But she had never been anything as cool as a dragon. *And this time I'm not even acting*, she reminded herself. *I really AM a dragon!*

Then another thought struck Mei. If she had a dragon-y face and dragon-y legs, she probably had a dragon-y tail. She turned to check. It was cool to have such a long neck! Sure enough, she had a long red tail with silver and gold embedded in its length, and an arrow tip.

That was when Mei spotted something even more exciting. Sprouting from her back was a pair of beautiful wings! Each wing was decorated with swirling patterns, and drops of silver and gold. She gave them a flap and... rose off the ground. Mei couldn't help but let out a cheer... and a red flame erupted from her mouth! The flame licked an apple hanging from a nearby branch. To Mei's surprise, the apple didn't burn. Instead, it transformed from a small, unripe fruit to one that was huge and juicy looking!

"Did I do that?" Mei wondered aloud, hovering in the air.

"You certainly did," said a voice. "Dragon Girls have special powers, after all."

Mei looked around, trying to figure out who had spoken. What was a Dragon Girl?

Climbing out of the reeds was a tiny pink creature with rounded ears, dark eyes and a pom-pom tail. It was like the fluffiest mouse Mei had ever seen.

"I'm Squeaklet," the creature announced, bowing deeply.

"Wow, you can talk!" Mei exclaimed. "I'm Mei. I've always wanted to meet a talking animal."

"What a coincidence! I've always wanted to meet a Treasure Dragon Girl," replied Squeaklet.

"I'm a Treasure Dragon Girl?" Mei repeated, her mind whirling.

"Yes! The Treasure Dragons protect this forest's most precious things," explained Squeaklet. Mei had so many questions, but Squeaklet spoke before she could ask them. "Are you going to do some more flying?"

"I don't really know *how* to," Mei admitted.

"It's not hard," said Squeaklet. "Just imagine you are using your wings to wave to a friend."

"Easy for you to say!" Mei laughed. "You don't have wings."

But Mei found that the tip actually worked. When she thought about waving her wings,

they fluttered to life. Mei rose off the ground again, and this time she went higher.

"That's it!" said Squeaklet, clapping his fluffy paws. "Now do it faster and with more power."

Mei gave it a shot. But one of her wings flapped quicker than the other and Mei veered to one side. Then she flapped her wings from front to back instead of up and down. She started to wonder if she would EVER get it right!

But Squeaklet didn't doubt her. "You've almost got it!" he called cheerfully as Mei toppled over on to the ground.

Mei groaned dramatically. "Maybe I'll just walk."

Squeaklet shook his fluffy head. "The Magic Forest is huge!"

"This is a *magic* forest?" Mei asked. The word *magic* made fireworks explode inside her.

"Of course! How many talking animals have you met in normal forests?" Squeaklet asked. "Now, we must hurry. The Tree Queen is waiting. She has a quest for you and the other Treasure Dragon Girls."

Mei couldn't hold back her questions any longer! "Who is the Tree Queen?" she asked. "What do you mean, a quest? And who are the others?"

"The sooner you learn to fly, the sooner you'll

find out," Squeaklet said, jumping on to Mei's shoulder. "Come on, try one more time."

Whenever Mei was in a play, she took a moment to focus before she went onstage. She did this now. *You are a Dragon Girl and you can fly*, she told herself. *You just need to believe it.*

The pep talk worked! The next time Mei

flapped her wings, she rose steadily into the air. She flapped again and shot forward. Soon she was going higher and faster than she'd ever thought possible.

"I knew you'd get the hang of it," Squeaklet called. "Follow me."

Squeaklet leapt off Mei's shoulder and on to a nearby treetop. From there, he leapt on to another tree, and so on. He was surprisingly fast! Mei could only just keep up.

"This is the best feeling EVER!" Mei whooped, skimming the treetops.

Finally, they came to a part of the forest where the trees thinned out. Beyond, Mei could see a beautiful glade. Surrounding it was a shimmering sphere of air. In the middle stood a tall, graceful tree. Sunlight fell in golden beams on to the bright grass. Mei really wanted to go in there.

"That is where the Tree Queen lives," Squeaklet explained. "You must enter the glade alone."

"Oh, please come too!" said Mei. She was already fond of the little guy.

"Don't worry. Whenever you need me, I'll be there," Squeaklet said. With a twitch of his downy tail, he disappeared.

Mei gazed at the shimmering air. It looked like some sort of force field. She longed to get into the glade, but she wasn't sure how. Gingerly, she reached out a paw. It went straight through! The air fizzed like when she added bath salts to her bath.

Taking a deep breath, Mei stepped through the force field and into the glade.

Inside the force field, the glade was even more beautiful. The colours were brighter, the sun more golden. Tiny metallic-winged insects flitted about. Jewel-coloured butterflies hovered around honey-scented flowers. A happy glow washed through Mei.

"Can you believe this place?"

"It's amazing, right?"

Mei jumped at the sound of the voices. There, in the middle of the glade, hovered two Dragon Girls. One was jade green and the other was sapphire blue. Like Mei, they had a heady mix of silver and gold on their wings and tails. They must be Treasure Dragon Girls, too!

"You two look incredible," exclaimed Mei. "And fierce. In a good way!"

The dragons laughed.

"Thanks!" said the one with sapphire-blue jewels embedded in her wings. "Is that you, Mei? It's me, Aisha. And this is Quinn. We just got here. Can you believe it? We're Dragon Girls!"

Mei stared at them, open-mouthed. Were

they really her friends from jewellery class? They looked so different.

Quinn let out a happy little roar. A wisp of green fire curled from her mouth. "I know! It's amazing!" she said. "Have you tried flying yet? It's kind of hard."

"So hard!" Aisha said, laughing. "I keep getting caught in my own tail! But I've figured out how to roar." She took a deep breath, opened her mouth, and let out a huge roar. Bright blue flames shot into the air.

Mei grinned. The dragons were definitely her friends Aisha and Quinn. She recognized their laughs. And their gemstones matched their friendship bracelets!

Mei looked around. "I was told to meet a Tree Queen here," she said. "Have you seen her yet?"

"No, there's no queen here. But there is this very impressive tree," said Aisha.

"It's incredible." Quinn nodded.

They gazed up at the majestic tree. Its strong branches reached towards the sky; its silvery leaves fluttered in the light.

As the three Dragon Girls watched, the tree began swaying. The branches softened into strong, graceful arMs.

"It's changing!" gasped Mei.

The tree's leaves turned into long, wavy hair, framing a beautiful, wise face. The tree's trunk became a flowing gown of mossy green.

"Welcome, Treasure Dragon Girls. I am the Tree Queen. I am glad to see you. The Magic Forest needs your help."

Pride surged through Mei. She was a Treasure Dragon in a magic forest! And she was needed! Nothing like this had ever happened to her before. She was going to enjoy every last minute of this adventure.

"Of course we'll help!" she declared.

"Yeah! We're not scared of anything!" Aisha added.

Mei noticed Quinn shuffling awkwardly, a nervous look on her face. *I bet she's braver than she realizes*, thought Mei.

The Tree Queen rustled her leaves as she spoke again. "Many years ago, the Shadow Queen was the ruler of the Magic Forest. With the help of her Shadow Sprites, she locked the Magic Forest into an endless grey twilight. Many of the forest's plants and animals struggled to survive without bright days to grow strong in the sunshine or dark nights to rest. The winters were harsh, and sometimes

lasted years. When the Shadow Queen was finally banished, I became queen. I've worked hard ever since to restore balance. But now her Shadow Sprites have returned. I can feel deep in my tree roots that she is gaining strength again."

Mei gulped. "But that's terrible!"

The Tree Queen nodded gravely. "The Shadow

Sprites have stolen three ancient objects from the forest's treasure vault deep underground. These objects are worth more than money. They are the source of the forest's magic! When these objects are removed from the vault, things quickly go wrong. This is terrible for the forest and all her creatures. Worse, if the objects stay out of the vault for too long, the problems can become permanent. You are the only ones who can return the treasure in time and restore the forest to harmony."

Mei knew she'd do whatever she could to find and return the missing treasure. How fantastic it would be to save the Magic Forest!

"But what if we can't find the treasure?"

Quinn asked, sounding worried. "This is all so new to us."

Aisha wrapped a wing around her. "Don't worry, Quinn. We'll do it together."

The Tree Queen smiled. "Exactly. And that is why you are the perfect team for this quest. The Shadow Sprites will make you doubt yourselves. But you are Dragon Girls, and you are stronger and smarter than them!"

Mei felt like she might burst. Hearing the Tree Queen say that made her feel like she really could do anything.

"Tell us what we need to do, and we'll do it," promised Mei.

"The first object you need to find is *The*

Forest Book," explained the Tree Queen.

"A *book*?" Mei said. She didn't think of books as treasure. She didn't love reading. Her mind often wandered and the words swam.

"This is no ordinary book, Mei," the Tree Queen explained. "It's a thousand years old. And it contains the entire history of the Magic Forest."

The Dragon Girls looked at one another in wonder.

The Tree Queen continued, "All the secrets of the forest are recorded in *The Forest Book*'s pages. The exact notes of birds' songs. The recipes for each flower's perfume. The favourite food of every animal. If the book isn't returned to the vault quickly, the plants and animals will forget how to behave and what to eat. The birds won't remember their songs, and the flowers will smell wrong. Even the rivers will forget to flow."

"We'll get the book back, don't worry," Mei promised.

She was rewarded with a broad smile. "Mei, you are in charge of this quest." The queen held out her long, branch-like arMs There was a soft bag on one, and on the other was a chain with some sort of object made of metal and studded with gemstones.

At first, Mei thought it was a clock. But then

she saw that it had only one hand. "A compass!" she said.

"Yes, a very old and powerful one," the Tree Queen explained. "But remember this: You can only ask it to help you one time during a quest. So make sure you use it wisely."

Mei slipped the chain over her head and fitted the bag across her chest. It blended into the metallic colours of her scales like a chameleon. "We'll be very careful," she promised.

"I know you will," said the Tree Queen. "You're Treasure Dragons, after all. Now, when you find the book, remember that it might have been bewitched. Who knows what the Shadow Sprites might have done to it!"

Mei looked at her friends. An adventure loomed. She was so glad they were going on it together!

"Goodbye, Treasure Dragons!" called the Tree Queen as she started turning back into a tree. "The birds tell me that Shadow Sprites were just sighted at Hoppy Hill. I suggest you start there."

Mei flapped her wings. "Great! Where's Hoppy H—"

But it was too late. The Tree Queen's wavy hair had turned back into leaves, her long arms into solid branches. Her wise face disappeared, and they were standing in front of a lovely but entirely normal-looking tree.

The Dragon Girls glanced at one another. *Did that really just happen?*

Together, they rose into the air and pushed through the glade's force field. Quinn and Aisha almost crashed into each other but, chuckling, they managed to avoid disaster. Watching her friends laugh at themselves made Mei feel better about her own troubles learning to fly.

"The more we do it, the better we'll become,"

she said, as much to herself as to Aisha and Quinn.

"So which way to Hoppy Hill, do you think?" asked Quinn as they hovered above the trees.

It was the million-pound question.

Just then, Mei saw a flash of movement. Something small, furry and very cute leapt from a branch and landed on her shoulder.

"Squeaklet!" Mei sighed. "You're here!"

"I am never far away," the little creature replied. "I'll show you the way to Hoppy Hill."

Soon the Treasure Dragons were soaring through the bright blue sky. Mei grinned. She knew that they had a huge task ahead of them, but it was so exciting to be here! The Magic

Forest unrolled like a gorgeous carpet beneath them, rich with colours and patterns.

Quinn flew up beside her. "Have you seen the trees?" she asked. "Some of them have blue leaves!"

Looking down, Mei saw that Quinn was right.

"This is a *magic* forest," Aisha pointed out,

flying up on the other side. "Maybe blue leaves are normal here?"

"There are some blue trees in the forest," Squeaklet confirmed. "They are called Sky Trees. But they don't grow here. The trees below are normally green."

"It must be because of the missing *Forest Book*!" Mei said. "I wonder if other things are going wrong, too?"

As she spoke, a flock of birds flew past them. They were flying upside down! The Treasure Dragon Girls exchanged a worried look. The Tree Queen had said that without *The Forest Book* safely in the vault, the plants and creatures would start forgetting how to behave. Was that happening to these birds?

"There's Hoppy Hill," Squeaklet called.

Up ahead was a hill blanketed in flowers and dotted with tiny alpine houses. Each hut had a sweet thatched roof made from bound-together straw.

"Time to land, Dragon Girls," Squeaklet called from his position on Mei's shoulder.

"This is so fun!" roared Aisha as they zoomed towards the hillside.

"The best!" Mei roared back.

"Umm, does anyone know how to land on the side of a hill?" asked Quinn.

Mei didn't have time to answer. The hill was coming up fast! She stuck out her paws, skidded, and did three messy somersaults before coming to a stop against a tree.

Mei had learned from acting that if you do something wrong onstage, you make it look like you did it on purpose. So she leapt to her paws and stood proud. She looked around for Squeaklet. She was pleased to see him safely perched on the branch of a nearby tree. He waved a paw at her, then disappeared into the foliage. Mei didn't mind. She knew he'd be back if she needed him.

Aisha and Quinn were lying in a tangled heap of shiny wings, claws and tails. Mei burst out laughing.

"It's all very well for *you* to laugh," said a cross voice. "But how would you like it if three huge dragons nearly wiped out your village?"

Mei looked left. She looked right. Then she looked down. Standing near one of the little houses was a very small, very fluffy bunny rabbit. The rabbit had soft ears, an orange puffball tail, and the grumpiest expression Mei had ever seen. The frowning face somehow made the rabbit even cuter.

Mei knelt down. "I'm sorry we scared you," she said. "We're new to flying, and definitely need to practise landing."

By now, other bunnies were hopping over. Each was grey with a different coloured tail, fluffy as a pom-pom.

"Apology accepted, I suppose," sniffed the rabbit, looking slightly less grumpy.

Quinn and Aisha untangled themselves and padded carefully over.

"We're actually here to help," Quinn explained.

"Help *how*?" asked a bunny with a pink tail.

"We're trying to stop the Shadow Sprites.

But to do that, we need to find a book," Quinn explained.

"A very powerful and important one," Aisha added.

The bunnies shook their heads and then waggled their fluffy bottoMs "We haven't seen any books," said a tiny bunny with an aqua tail. "And sorry, but we can't help you look right now. We keep losing things ourselves."

"What things?" asked Mei.

"Words, mostly," said the bunny. "We can't remember the names of things, or what they're for."

Mei felt her insides pinch. They had already

seen blue leaves and birds flying upside down. Now bunnies were forgetting things!

The bunny pointed her paw at a pile of carrots. "Do you know what those things are? We keep digging them up, but we can't remember why."

Some of the bunnies had laid the carrots out as if they were benches and were trying to sit on them. But they kept rolling off and landing with their fluffy tails in the air. Some of the older bunnies were using the carrots as walking sticks, but they weren't quite the right height. Some of the younger bunnies were using them like swords, to play-fight. Others were trying to juggle carrots, but they were

much too big for the bunnies, so carrots were rolling all over the place.

"They're carrots!" Mei said. "You *eat* them."

The bunnies looked at her, eyes narrowed. "How do you know they're not poisonous?"

Mei reached out and grabbed a carrot,

munching on it happily. "See? Delicious!"

A bunny with an aqua tail sniffed at the carrot. He took a nibble. "The Dragon Girl is right. These are extremely tasty!"

The other bunnies hopped over to the pile of carrots and began to crunch away. "They're fantastic!" they exclaimed, noses waffling with pleasure.

"If the bunnies have forgotten they like carrots, then things are really serious," said Quinn softly.

Mei nodded in agreement.

Aisha said what they were all thinking. "We have to find *The Forest Book* quickly."

Mei looked around, but all she could see

were flowers, a few small trees, and the tiny huts with their roofs made of straw and grass.

Hang on! There was something strange about one of the huts. Its roof was made from something smooth and brown, with golden corners.

Mei's heart thudded. "That hut has a book as its roof!" she whispered to Quinn and Aisha.

"You're right!" said Aisha. "Is it *The Forest Book*?"

"It *has* to be!" said Quinn. "Look! I think I see trees on the cover. What should we do? We can't just rip it off."

"Let's ask for it," said Mei. "The bunnies will understand how important this is."

"Excuse me!" Mei called to the rabbits, who were still munching on carrots. She pointed to the hut with the book roof. "Whose hut is this?"

The little bunny with the bright pink tail looked up. "Mine. Isn't the new roof great?"

"Where did you get it?" asked Aisha.

"It was all very strange. One day we woke up and the entire village was covered in shadows."

As the bunny spoke, all the others covered their eyes with their long fluffy ears. Clearly just thinking about that day was scary. The Dragon Girls exchanged a look. It sounded like the Shadow Sprites had been here.

"When the shadows cleared away," continued the bunny, "my hut had a brand-new roof!"

All the listening bunnies stuck up their ears again and cheered.

"The thing is, it's not actually a roof. We think it's *The Forest Book*," Mei explained gently. "It was taken from the Magic Forest's treasure vault. With *The Forest Book* missing, the plants and animals are all confused. That's why you keep forgetting things, like what carrots are. I am very sorry, but we must return it to the vault."

"No. You canNOT take my lovely roof!" said the bunny firmly.

The bunnies hopped over and surrounded the hut, linking their paws and glaring at Mei. Some of them even growled.

"What do we do?" Quinn whispered, looking worried.

"We are stronger than the bunnies," said Aisha. "We could grab the book and fly away. But that's too mean! We'd be no better than the Shadow Sprites."

Mei had an idea. "Let's create a replacement

roof! We're good at making things. We could create something the bunnies will really treasure."

The others agreed that this was a great plan.

Nearby, long golden-green reeds grew along a stream. Mei picked a handful and then wrapped another reed around the bunch to hold them together. *Perfect!* She picked more reeds and tied these to the first bunch.

Aisha held up a long purple feather she'd found. "How about we weave this in?" she suggested.

"Yes!" agreed Mei. "Let's make this roof as gorgeous as possible."

Aisha and Quinn ran around, collecting

reeds and feathers and flowers for Mei to weave into the roof. The bunnies paid them no attention. They were too busy working their way through the carrots.

Finally, Mei took a step back. "It's done! What do you think?"

Quinn tilted her head. "It's good," she said. "But I feel like it's missing something."

Aisha nodded. "This roof has to be *amazing* if those bunnies are going to give up the book."

What could they add? They had woven in the prettiest flowers and feathers they could find.

"We could add some carrots," Aisha suggested.

Quinn laughed. "Then the bunnies will eat their roof! We need to make it something they'll treasure, not snack on."

Quinn's words made Mei think. They were Treasure Dragons, so they were good at finding treasure – and they were good at protecting it. But could it mean something else as well? She thought about when she'd first arrived in the forest. The red flame from her roar had made the unripe apple juicy and gorgeous.

"I have an idea," she said. "Let's try roaring together over the roof."

Aisha's eyes sparkled. "Let's do it."

The three Treasure Dragons gathered around the thatched roof they'd made. "One, two, three, ROAR!" cried Mei.

Mei's red flame mingled in the air with Quinn's jade-green flame and Aisha's sapphire one. The swirling colours floated down towards the roof. Mei held her breath as the flames touched the reeds. She really hoped all their hard work wasn't about to go up in smoke!

Quinn gasped. "It's changing!"

The reeds now glowed a gorgeous bright gold. The flowers glittered like jewels. The purple feathers looked the same, but when Mei touched one, she found it had turned hard, like metal. The whole roof had transformed into a bejewelled masterpiece.

"What have you got there?" called a bunny,

hopping over. His eyes lit up when he saw the roof. "That's beautiful. Is it for us?"

"We were going to give it to you in exchange for the book. But you don't want another roof, do you?" Mei said sweetly.

"Yes, we do! We do!" cried the bunnies, hopping closer and leaping up and down excitedly. "You can have that ugly brown roof. We never liked it anyway. This one is MUCH nicer."

Mei pretended to look unsure. Then she let out a dramatic sigh. "OK, you can have this new one. We'll even install it for you."

Very carefully, she removed the book from the top of the hut. Then Mei, Quinn and Aisha picked up the new roof and lowered it into position. It fit perfectly! The bunnies hopped around, stamping their feet in delight.

"That's the best roof in the Magic Forest!" they sang joyfully.

Mei looked at the book in her paws. They had already succeeded in the first part of their task! And it hadn't been too difficult! She felt a shiver just holding this book. For the first time, she could understand why some people loved books so much. It was amazing to think about all the stories and secrets contained within this leather cover.

"Can we take a little peek inside?" pleaded Quinn.

Mei nodded. She was curious, too. But when

she opened the cover, she groaned. The book was entirely blank! "Maybe it's not *The Forest Book* after all?"

"But the title says it's *The Forest Book*," Quinn pointed out.

"And it's so big and grand," Aisha added. "This must be it. And remember, the Tree Queen said

the Shadow Sprites might have cast a spell on it. Maybe they took out the words and hid them somewhere else?"

Mei turned to the bunnies. "Do you remember the Shadow Sprites doing anything to the book?" she asked urgently.

"What are Shadow Sprites?" asked one bunny.

"What's a book?" asked another.

Mei sighed. "They're not going to be able to help us."

"You should talk to the Book Butterflies," said Squeaklet, appearing suddenly and landing lightly on Mei's shoulder. "They know everything about books."

Mei rubbed Squeaklet between the ears. It was good to see the little guy again.

"Book Butterflies? Where do we find them?" she asked.

"They live in a meadow not far away," Squeaklet said.

Mei tucked *The Forest Book* into the bag the Tree Queen had given her. Even though the book was big, it hardly made a lump inside the bag. "So, what are we waiting for?" Mei grinned at her friends. "Let's fly!"

The Treasure Dragons waved goodbye to the bunnies, who were too busy admiring their new roof and chomping on carrots to wave back.

"Fly straight ahead," instructed Squeaklet. "You'll know when you're in the right place." With a swish of fur, he disappeared into the treetops.

Mei patted *The Forest Book* in her bag and they zoomed off, weaving around trees laden with jewel-like fruit. They whooshed across a field of wildflowers growing on the edge of a mountain, flying so low that the blooms brushed against Mei's scales.

"You're covered in pollen!" Aisha laughed, copying Mei until she, too, was dotted with pollen.

"It looks like gold dust," Quinn called.

"We're Treasure Dragons, so that fits!" Mei called back.

A few moments later, the Dragon Girls found themselves flying through some sort of storm cloud. A thick greyness surrounded them. Mei

coughed, and her eyes felt gritty. She couldn't see her friends anywhere. Even worse, Mei felt confused. *What are we doing again?* she wondered. *Where are we going?* She shook her head, trying to clear her thoughts. *Keep it together,* she told herself sternly. *We're going to find the Book Butterflies.*

But now Mei felt unsure about their

plan. What if there was no such thing as a Book Butterfly? Then she wondered if the book they'd found *was* the right one. She desperately needed to clear her throat again, but she hardly had the strength to cough.

Mei's stomach dropped. *Wait! This is no storm cloud. These are Shadow Sprites!*

As Mei watched, the grey shadowy particles joined together until they formed bigger, even more sinister shapes. Soon the air was filled with menacing shadows, shifting in strange snake-like patterns.

Mei knew what she had to do. Taking a deep breath, she opened her mouth and let out a ROAR. A red flame erupted from her mouth and cleared a bright, sparkling path in the grey cloud. Mei could see her friends! They, too, were blinking away the shadowy confusion caused by the Shadow Sprites.

"We have to get away from here!" Mei roared to Aisha and Quinn. "Follow me!"

Mei began to fly along the path her roar had created. Aisha and Quinn stuck close behind. As she charged past the Shadow Sprites, Mei felt a breeze on her face. It smelled like sunshine.

We'll get through this, Mei told herself. The thought made the last of the shadowy doubt disappear. Mei felt confident and strong once more.

"Phew! That was horrible!" Quinn groaned.

"The worst! Hey, where is that breeze coming from?" Aisha called.

Mei saw movement in a meadow down below. Were they flowers blowing in the wind? No! It was the fluttering of thousands of butterfly wings in every possible colour. Each butterfly wing was streaked with gold.

"Yes!" Mei cried. "That's where we're headed!"

A moment later, the three Treasure Dragons landed softly. The meadow was near the side of a cliff, and down below raged a wild river. The Dragon Girls were a little dusty, but more than anything, they felt relieved to be away from the Shadow Sprites.

Butterflies perched on a log nearby. They read from tiny books made from leaves and flower petals. A soft, papery scent rose from their fluttering wings.

An orange-and-gold butterfly glanced up from her book and smiled. "You must be Dragon Girls!" she said in a soft, flittering voice. "I've read about you."

"Yes, we're Treasure Dragon Girls," Mei said proudly. "And you must be the Book Butterflies. We're so glad to find you. We really need your help."

"Sorry, we can't help anyone right now," replied a pink-and-gold butterfly, using an antenna to turn the page in her book. "We've got enough problems of our own. Our tree is covered in strange caterpillars! We're researching what to do."

"But you were all caterpillars once," said Mei. *Had the butterflies forgotten?*

"Yes, but we never did yoga like these ones," said another butterfly, fluttering her blue-and-gold wings.

"Caterpillars doing yoga?" Mei and her friends looked at one another. Even in the Magic Forest, that sounded weird!

The butterflies all nodded. "Come, we'll show you!"

They closed their tiny books and flew towards the tree. The butterflies looked like a stream of colourful confetti.

As they got closer, Mei saw tiny black shapes moving across the tree's trunk. They didn't look like any caterpillars she'd ever seen. And Mei's mum did yoga, but she never made those shapes! In fact, the shapes looked more like...

"They're words, not caterpillars!" she cried. Mei tried to read the writing, but the letters were all jumbled. Some were upside down, others were back to front. It was impossible to make any sense of them. "They must be the missing words!"

"You know about *The Forest Book*?" sighed the blue butterfly. "The most precious treasure of all!"

"We don't just *know* about it," said Aisha. "We have it!"

Mei pulled it from her bag and held it up.

"Oh my!" The pink butterfly flew closer. "I've always wanted to read *The Forest Book*."

"That's the problem," said Mei, showing them the blank pages within.

The butterflies gasped in horror.

"It's terrible, I know," Mei said. "But at least we've found the words now! Can you help us get them back into the book?"

"Oh yes, we can do that easily," said the orange butterfly.

"GREAT!" cried Mei, Aisha and Quinn.

The blue butterfly twitched her antennae. "But first, you need to pass a test. We must be sure you are trustworthy."

"Of course we're trustworthy!" Aisha replied hotly.

"The Tree Queen herself sent us," Mei added.

"Then the test will be easy for you," chorused the Book Butterflies.

Without waiting to explain, the butterflies

rose into the air and began to loop and spin like figure skaters gliding over ice.

"Look, they're writing something!" Quinn cried.

Elegant gold letters trailed behind the little creatures, as if written by an invisible hand. A sentence shimmered in the air:

Books are butterflies with stories on their wings.

"Lovely!" Mei sighed.

The Book Butterflies hovered in mid-air

beside the glowing words. "Now it's your turn."

Mei felt her stomach flip. "What do you mean?"

"Write something beautiful for us," said the orange butterfly.

"And perfect," added the blue one.

Perfect? "Um, Quinn or Aisha, do you want to try?" Mei asked, turning to her friends.

"No, you are carrying the book. You must do it," the butterflies said firmly.

"I don't know what to write," Mei groaned.

"Don't think too hard about it," Quinn said. "Just listen to your heart."

"My heart is beating too fast for me to hear anything," Mei grumbled.

"You're a Treasure Dragon," Aisha reassured her. "You'll come up with something that really shines."

Mei loved that her friends believed in her. But she wasn't so sure.

Then Quinn made a great suggestion. "Pretend the sky is a stage and you are doing a performance."

Instantly, Mei's nerves dropped away. She always felt brave onstage. Mei flapped her wings and shot smoothly into the air. Using the tip of her tail, she began to trace out words in the air. When she'd finished, Mei watched the sky anxiously.

"The words aren't appearing," she said. "Did I

do something wrong?"

"Maybe we need to do something extra?" Aisha suggested. "Like a group roar!"

Of course! Mei nodded, and her friends rose into the air to join her. Together they roared until the air was filled with red, green and blue flames. The flames swirled and looped around one another like the ribbons gymnasts sometimes danced with.

Mei held her breath as the bright flames flicked over the invisible words. Like the first star appearing in the night sky, Mei's words began to twinkle.

"It's working!" Aisha cheered, doing a flip in the air.

Mei grinned as more words appeared. She hoped she hadn't made any spelling mistakes!

Our wings are strong, our hearts are bold,

but best of all our words are gold.

Quinn and Aisha beamed as they read Mei's sentence.

"It even rhymes!" said Aisha, giving Mei a paw bump.

The Book Butterflies fluttered around, chattering quietly before turning to Mei.

"Well done, Treasure Dragon!" they twittered. "We asked you to do something difficult and you didn't let us down. That proves you are trustworthy. We will help you put the words back into *The Forest Book*."

The Book Butterflies began to beat their wings. The leaves rustled, filling the air with their papery smell. The mixed-up letters on the tree started to quiver. Then, one by one, they peeled off the leaves and the branches. Suddenly the sky was full of strange letters – a whole book's worth! The letters quivered in the air.

The Book Butterflies looked puzzled.

"The words should have settled on the pages of *The Forest Book*. They must have a spell on them!" said the red butterfly.

"Of course! That's why we can't read the writing!" exclaimed the blue butterfly.

Mei and her friends studied the mysterious letters hanging in the air above them. Mei was desperate to undo the spell so she could read all the Magic Forest's secrets. Usually reading was the last thing Mei wanted to do.

But she wanted to read this book more than anything in the world! *Mum would be proud*, she thought.

Mei flapped her wings and rose into the air. She reached out and touched the strange letters. They swayed like branches in the wind. Mei started rearranging the letters closest to her, turning them the right way up and trying them in a different order to make words. It was fun, hovering in the air and rearranging letters. Like playing Scrabble, but in the sky!

Soon the three Dragon Girls were flying around, calling out ideas and bumping into one another to reach different letters. But whenever they switched around the order of the letters – or turned them the right way up – the letters simply jumped back to where they'd been.

Mei was feeling very frustrated. "Argh!" she roared, letting out a puff of ruby-coloured smoke and flopping on to the grass below for a break. "It's no good."

"Look!" Quinn gasped.

The word *FOREST* hung in the air.

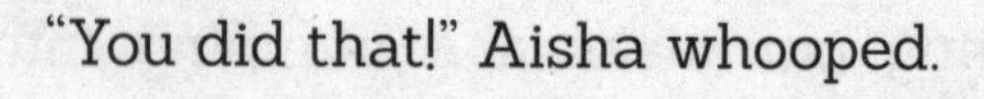

"You did that!" Aisha whooped.

"I did?" Mei was confused.

"Well, your roar did," Quinn explained. "When

that puff of smoke touched the letters, they changed."

"Quick, do it again!" Aisha said, her brown eyes flashing.

Mei shot into the air, fizzing with energy again. She took a deep breath and roared loudly. Sure enough, when her ruby smoke flowed across the letters, they moved around into words she could read:

Welcome to The Forest Book*! Come, my reader, please take a look. Inside are all our secrets true...*

But the rest of the words were still enchanted. This was going to take a lot of roaring if each roar only worked on a few lines! Unless...

"Guys, what if it's not *my* roar that breaks the spell," Mei said to her friends. "But rather, *our* roars that do? On the count of three, let's do our biggest roars ever. OK?"

Aisha and Quinn nodded, as Mei shouted, "One, two, THREE!"

The Treasure Dragons rose high into the air and roared as one. The sound was so powerful it swayed the trees and made the air shimmer. Red, green and blue flames swirled in a glorious twist of light that got brighter as it spun closer to Mei.

Then... *Wham!* The wall of light and sound slammed against Mei, knocking her sideways. Suddenly, she was spinning through the air. She couldn't tell up from down. *What is happening? Where are the others?* Mei tried to open her eyes, but the flashes of light blinded her.

Her vision cleared just in time to see *The Forest Book*... tumbling through the air! Mei reached out to grab it, but instead crashed into the tree at the edge of the cliff.

Mei was dizzy from the crash, and her wings felt all crumpled. Then she saw something terrible: *The Forest Book* was tumbling over the cliff's edge. *There's a river down there!* There was NO WAY she was going to let the book be destroyed.

Mei flapped with all her might and rose into the air. *The Forest Book* had already disappeared from view. Mei flew to the cliff's edge. There was the book, falling fast! Mei zoomed down towards it. Almost! Again she tried, but still the book was just out of reach of her talons.

"NO!" Mei roared . . . and she shot forward.

Her roar gave her extra power! She roared

again and lunged at the falling book with her added speed. She managed to grip it with one claw.

"Got you!" cried Mei, holding the book in the air as she tumbled into the water.

The churn of white water swirled around Mei, dragging her down. She held *The Forest Book* up over her head and kicked with all her might. She was determined to keep the book dry. It would be terrible if it were destroyed by water. But how to get out of the raging current? There was no way she was strong enough to fly up and out of the water.

"We've got you, Mei!" called a voice.

The air above filled with blue and green smoke as Quinn and Aisha whooshed down towards Mei. Quinn scooped a paw under

her left wing, and Aisha took the right one. Together, they lifted Mei from the water and carried her to the riverbank.

"Is *The Forest Book* OK?" Mei asked, trying to catch her breath.

"It's fine!" said Aisha, taking it from Mei and inspecting it. There were a couple of splashes on the cover, but that was all.

"You did great, Mei." Quinn smiled.

Mei had never felt so relieved! She was exhausted, but she had enough energy to give her friends the biggest wing hugs ever.

"Thanks, guys," she said. "That roar of ours literally blew me away!"

"Wasn't it awesome?" said Aisha, her eyes

sparkling. "I'm only just getting my head around how powerful we are."

"Especially when we work together," added Quinn. "But one thing's worrying me. Did the words end up back in the book?"

Mei held her breath as she opened *The Forest Book*. What if the words weren't there? But looking down, she saw they had succeeded. There were words on the page, and she could read them! She flicked to the first chapter.

The Magic Forest has been blooming since the beginning of time. The magic in the soil is so strong, every single flower, tree and animal has special powers.

"We did it!" Aisha whooped. "Now we just need to—"

Aisha was cut short by an angry buzzing sound. Looking up, the Treasure Dragons saw hundreds of tiny grey dots in the air above them.

"Are they insects?" Quinn whispered.

"I don't think so," Mei muttered back.

She had a bad feeling. The feeling got worse as the little dots joined together to form a huge grey streak. It lashed back and forth overhead, like the tail of an angry cat.

"Shadow Sprites!" Aisha yelled. "They're after the book!"

"Well, they're not getting it!" Mei declared.

She tucked the book back into her bag and the Treasure Dragons rose into the air. The Shadow Sprites whipped around them, making everything darker and colder.

For a moment, the familiar doubt began to creep in. *You'll never beat the Shadow Sprites. So much for being a Treasure Dragon – you can't even protect an old book!*

Mei tried to block out the dark thoughts, reminding herself they weren't true. She opened her mouth and roared, filling the air with red smoke. Aisha and Quinn joined in, and the sound of their roars echoed off the rocky cliff face. It sounded like there were a hundred dragons roaring!

The grey, shadowy forms swirling around them were swamped by the colourful, powerful smoke. Before long, the Shadow Sprites had seeped away to nothing.

The Dragon Girls landed back on the ground beside the river.

"Look!" Quinn exclaimed.

Mei looked down at the book. It was glowing, as though it had a light inside. And then she noticed something else that was glowing, too. The silver and gold that decorated their wings and tails!

"We really *are* Treasure Dragons!" Mei sighed happily.

"Better make sure the book is still OK," Aisha urged.

Mei pulled the book out and opened it. *Phew!* The words were still there. Even better, illustrations had now appeared. There were drawings of golden vines, ripe fruit and delicate flowers. Magical-looking birds nestled on the vines. Mei was sure she saw one of them flutter its wings! Without a doubt, this was the most extraordinary book she had ever seen. It was clear her friends thought so, too.

"I know we need to get going," Quinn said, "but can we read just a few pages first?"

"I think we deserve a little break after all that excitement," Aisha added.

"You bet we do!" Mei said.

So together, the Treasure Dragons began to read about the Magic Forest. They learned about the different creatures who lived there, and how the Tree Queen had been the forest's guardian for centuries. There was even an adorable drawing of her when she was a tiny sapling! They also read about the evil Shadow Queen, and how she was always trying to take control of the forest.

Mei was so absorbed she didn't notice when Squeaklet landed lightly on her shoulder.

"You need to return the book to the vault," Squeaklet said, giving Mei a furry nudge. "If you leave it too long, the plants and animals might forget how to be themselves. Forever."

Hurriedly, Mei put the book away, and she and the others leapt to their paws.

"Which way?" Quinn asked.

Mei looked at Squeaklet. "Do you know where the vault is?"

Squeaklet shook his head. "It's a closely guarded secret."

"What about the compass the Tree Queen gave you?" Aisha said. "We can only use it once, but maybe now is the time?"

Mei had completely forgotten about the compass dangling from her neck! It seemed to shine more brightly now, like it wanted her to ask a question. She lifted it up gently with one paw. "Which way to the Forest Vault?" she asked.

The little hand swung around until it pointed east.

Mei looked at Quinn and Aisha. "Ready to fly?"

The words had barely left her mouth when her friends took off. Of course they were ready! It was late in the afternoon, and the golden sunshine bathed the forest in a warm glow.

Mei did a loop in the air, while Squeaklet held on very tightly. It felt so good to be here, especially now that they had broken the spell on *The Forest Book*!

Quinn and Aisha joined in with the acrobatics. Mei could have kept flying forever, but soon she felt the compass tug gently at its chain. The little arrow was now pointing straight down.

"Time to land!" Mei called, and the Treasure Dragons glided smoothly down to the ground.

They landed in a part of the forest where the trees grew thick and tall. It was dark, and a chilly wind whistled through fallen leaves. The plants smelled funny. It reminded Mei of burnt toast. She frowned. Clearly, the Magic Forest was still not quite right. They needed to get *The Forest Book* back into the vault immediately!

"Where's the vault?" Aisha asked.

Mei had been wondering the same thing.

"Here," said a sad, gravelly voice.

On Mei's shoulder, Squeaklet jumped in surprise. No wonder: peeking out from thick ivy was a big face made of . . . rock? Ivy trailed across it like a green curtain.

Mei looked at the stone face in wonder. "Did you just speak?"

"Yes," said Stone Face. It had a big, bulbous nose and eyes that looked a bit teary. "I am the keeper of the vault. But I haven't been doing a very good job of it lately. And it's lonely here, especially now that the soldier ants won't talk to me any more."

"Why is that?" asked Mei.

A pebble tear rolled down its face, landing noisily on the ground.

"They're angry that I let things be stolen from the vault." Stone Face sighed. "But the Shadow Queen and her sprites tricked me!" Pebble tears started rolling rapidly and noisily down his stone cheeks.

"Don't cry!" Quinn said kindly. "Mei, show him what we've got."

The moment Mei held up *The Forest Book*, Stone Face stopped crying. His mouth stretched into such a wide smile, Mei was worried he might crack!

"You found it!" He beamed. "Things have been so strange without that book in the vault. The trees don't know if it's winter or summer. And the soldier ants keep forgetting how to march. I saw them doing the cha-cha earlier. I mean, it's great that they're learning how to dance, but they're supposed to help me protect the vault. Now the forest can return to normal! Tell me, are you Dragon Girls?"

"Yes, we're Treasure Dragon Girls," Aisha said.

Stone Face whistled, looking impressed.

"So, could you open the vault, please?" Mei asked politely.

"Sure," said Stone Face. "When you say what you're meant to say."

"What do you mean? Is there a password?" Quinn asked. She looked worried.

Stone Face scrunched up his nose, sending sand and small pebbles flying. "It's not exactly a password. But I can't just let anyone in. From now on, I can only open if I am sure you mean well." Stone Face looked at the Dragon Girls.

"You seem kind and brave. But you still have to say what you're meant to say."

Mei turned to Quinn and Aisha. "Any ideas?"

"Open sesame?" Aisha suggested.

Stone Face raised his eyebrows. "This isn't some fairy tale," he said a little sternly.

That gave Mei an idea. "Maybe there's something in here," she said, opening *The Forest Book* to a random page. When she read what was written there, she gasped.

"Look!" Mei cried, showing the page to the others. Aisha and Quinn leaned over and read the words.

"Maybe there's something in here," she said, opening The Forest Book *at a random page.*

When she read what was written there,

she gasped.

Quinn frowned. "That's what just happened."

Mei nodded. "The book is writing our quest as we go!"

"No way!" Aisha yelped. "Let me see."

As she spoke, curly lettering appeared on the page:

"No way!" Aisha yelped. "Let me see."

"That's so magical," Quinn marvelled, watching as new words appeared. "But we still don't know how to open the vault."

"Or maybe we do," said Mei, flying over to Stone Face. She held out *The Forest Book*. "Is the story of how the Shadow Queen tricked you in here?" she asked gently.

Stone Face began to cry again. "Yes! I will be forever remembered as the one who allowed treasure to be stolen."

"But the story isn't finished yet," Mei pointed out. "If you let us in, you'll be known as the one who put things right again."

This made Stone Face sob even louder. "How do I know you're not tricking me?" he wailed.

She held *The Forest Book* tightly and closed her eyes. Mei needed Stone Face to understand. They wanted to protect the Magic Forest's

treasure as much as he did! Mei felt a warm glow in her scales. She opened her eyes and saw that her red gemstones were glowing. That *had* to be a good sign.

Mei turned to the most recent page and held it out to Stone Face. "Read this," she said.

In his deep, gravelly voice, Stone Face read:

Mei needed Stone Face to understand. They wanted to protect the Magic Forest's treasure as much as he did!

"Do you really?" Stone Face asked Mei.

"The words wouldn't have appeared in *The Forest Book* if they weren't true," Mei pointed out.

"That's right!" said Stone Face, cracking another huge grin. "Stand aside, Dragon Girls!"

There was a rumbling noise like distant thunder as Stone Face swung himself open, revealing a dark space that led into the mountain. Mei, Aisha and Quinn peered in excitedly. *What was in there?*

"Careful!" Squeaklet said suddenly. "Danger nearby!"

Mei felt something brush against her. She saw a flash of grey. A Shadow Sprite was trying to wrap itself around *The Forest Book*! Mei knew if she paused even for a moment, the sprite would make her doubt herself again.

"Don't you dare!" Mei roared, swiping a claw at the sprite.

With an annoyed hiss, it dissolved into dust.

"Into the vault, quickly!" called Stone Face. "I must shut the door behind you!"

Mei stepped through first, Squeaklet on her shoulder. Aisha and Quinn followed and the door rumbled closed.

Mei and her friends waited for their eyes to adjust to the gloom. A tunnel stretched before them, leading deep into the belly of the earth. Mei had been expecting a dark and scary tunnel, but in fact it was dotted with beautiful lamps set high up on the walls. As the Treasure Dragons passed, the lamps lit up one by one, each a different colour. Glowing circles of light twinkled.

After a few moments, the tunnel widened, and suddenly they were in a cavernous hall. It must have been four storeys high and as wide as a stadium. Treasure glittered on every surface! On one side they could see thick gold chains looped across the walls of the vault,

many of them dripping in gemstones. Another corner was given over to goblets and statues and delicate vases of every shape and size. The floor was strewn with ancient coins and even more twinkling gemstones.

Mei and the others sighed happily. What an extraordinary sight!

"Where should we put *The Forest Book*?" Aisha asked.

"I feel like it needs to go somewhere special," Quinn said.

Mei looked around. Towards the back of the vault were three empty columns, about waist height. On the side of each column was a name plate. She padded closer to read them.

The first one read *Magic Mirror*, and the second read *Heartstring Violin*. On the final plate were the words *The Forest Book*.

She took *The Forest Book* from the bag and flipped to the most recent page.

Mei was sad to give up The Forest Book. *It was the best book she had ever read. On the other hand, she was happy that she and her friends had done so well on their quest.*

Mei read this out loud to Quinn and Aisha, laughing. "Sometimes I think the book is telling me how to feel."

A new line appeared in *The Forest Book*. Mei, Aisha and Quinn read it together.

The Forest Book *was grateful to Mei and her friends for helping out. It hoped that they would come and read it again sometimes – because a book that never gets read is a sad book indeed.*

"Of COURSE we'll come and read you again!" Aisha said.

"We're part of one another's stories now," Quinn added.

"And that bonds us for life!" Mei finished, stroking the well-worn cover as she returned it to its rightful place on the column. "You are by far the best book I've ever read," she told it. "And I'm not just saying that because I'm in it!"

A roar began building up inside Mei. She and her friends had just finished their first ever quest! It hadn't been easy, but that made Mei feel even prouder. The roar inside her grew and grew until she couldn't hold it in any longer. Aisha and Quinn joined in the gleeful roaring. The vault swirled with even more colours than before.

Mei felt something snuffle at her neck. "Quit it, Squeaklet!" she giggled. "Your whiskers are tickling me."

"Sorry, but it's time to return to the Tree Queen," Squeaklet told her. He gave her neck another whiskery tickle, then scampered to his spot on her shoulder.

Mei and her friends took one last glance at the treasure before retracing their steps along the tunnel.

At the vault's entrance, Mei called, "Stone Face, please open the door!"

The vault's entrance slid open and the last of the day's sunshine flooded in.

The Treasure Dragons padded outside. "I'm happy that we completed the quest," Aisha said, "but I'm sad to leave. I loved looking at all that treasure!"

"Same," agreed Mei. "It's not that I need to *own* all those beautiful things. I just want to gaze at them."

"Exactly!" Quinn joined in. "It's like feeling

the warmth of the sun on your face."

"Yup! You three are definitely Treasure Dragons!" Stone Face chuckled. "Great work getting the book back where it belongs. I can already see its effect."

A line of soldier ants marched past in perfect formation.

"It's good that they've remembered how to march," Mei said, "but I'd like to see them doing the cha-cha."

The very last ant in the line did a quick hip wiggle and flung one of its six arms to the side. "We haven't forgotten how to dance!" it called up at Mei. "We have dance class soon. Join us?"

"Next time," promised Mei. "Right now we have to head back to the Tree Queen. Goodbye, ants. Goodbye, Stone Face."

"Bye, Dragon Girls," called Stone Face. "I'll be seeing you again soon."

Squeaklet nuzzled Mei's face and then jumped down lightly. "I'll see you again, too," he said.

"You're not coming?" Mei asked. "How will we find our way to the glade?"

"You'll find it," Squeaklet said confidently. "Head towards the sunset. And don't worry; I am never far away."

The Treasure Dragons flapped their mighty wings and launched into the sky. The air was cool as it brushed against their shimmering scales like fresh water.

Together, the three friends looped and twirled through the pink-and-orange sky. They enjoyed their sunset flight so much that Mei was almost sorry when she spotted the glade down below. But she was excited to see the Tree Queen again.

"Last one there is an empty treasure chest!" Aisha shouted, swooping towards the glade.

"Hey!" laughed Mei, speeding up. "No fair!"

"No way am I going to be last!" declared Quinn, flapping her wings as hard as she could.

A moment later, the Treasure Dragons

tumbled on to the velvety mint-green grass of the glade.

"That was quite an entrance!" laughed the Tree Queen in her warm way.

"Oops, sorry!" said Mei, jumping up quickly. Landing in a heap probably wasn't the best way to appear before the queen of the Magic Forest.

But the Tree Queen didn't seem to mind. "Well done, Treasure Dragons. I already know you've succeeded because the plants and animals are returning to normal. I couldn't be more grateful!"

The Treasure Dragons beamed at one another.

"What do you need us to do now?" Mei asked. She was ready for anything.

"I need you to return to your homes," said the Tree Queen. "Your friends and families will miss you if you stay here any longer."

"Oh," said Mei. She didn't want to leave this magical place yet!

"You three must get some rest," continued the queen, her brown eyes twinkling.

The Treasure Dragons looked at her hopefully.

"Because I will require your help again soon," explained the queen. "As you know, the Shadow Sprites have stolen two other iteMs The Magic Mirror and the Heartstring Violin need to be returned to the vault. They won't be easy to retrieve. The quests might even be dangerous. Are you willing to return?"

Mei, Aisha and Quinn didn't need to look at one another to know the answer to that.

"Of course!" they chorused.

The Tree Queen's smile broadened. "I hoped you'd say that."

Quinn raised a paw. "How do we get back?"

"I will show you," said the Tree Queen.

Mei handed the compass and the magic bag back to the Tree Queen, who said she'd keep them both safe until they returned.

Then the Tree Queen began to sway back and forth, dropping three objects from her branches. Mei's friendship bracelet landed in front of her. Mei saw that Aisha's and Quinn's bracelets had fallen near them.

"I was looking into the red bead of my bracelet when I first arrived," Mei said.

The Tree Queen nodded. "These are your travel charMs They guide you into the Magic Forest, and home again," she explained. "Wear them at all times. They will let you know when I need you again. Goodbye for now, Treasure Dragons."

With a rustle of her leaves, the Tree Queen turned back into a normal tree.

Mei, Aisha and Quinn smiled at one another. The adventures had only just begun!

"See you at jewellery class!" Mei said to the others.

Mei gazed into the bead in the centre of her bracelet. She could see shapes deep in the red glass. She looked closer. Yes! There was the community centre, where the jewellery class was held. Mei found herself spinning around and around, ever faster. The scene grew larger, unfolding around her. The golden light of the forest sunset faded, and Mei smelled the crisp freshness of snow. She closed her eyes and softly chanted:

Magic Forest, Magic Forest, come explore.
Magic Forest, Magic Forest, hear my roar!

When Mei opened her eyes, the forest had vanished entirely. She was back in the community centre.

The door opened and in walked her teacher. "You look like you're a thousand miles away," Ms Ahmed laughed.

"I kind of was." Mei smiled.

"You finished your mum's necklace!" Ms Ahmed sounded impressed.

Looking down at her workspace, Mei saw the necklace was indeed finished. On either side of the pretty bead were tiny golden leaves threaded on to the metal chain. They looked exactly like the Tree Queen's leaves! Mei picked up the necklace. It was beautiful. And she could have sworn the metal leaves rustled.

"Your mum is waiting out front," said Ms Ahmed, drawing the blinds. "Good job, Mei.

You got a lot done today."

"Thanks, Ms Ahmed," said Mei, grabbing her things.

She had done even more than Ms Ahmed realized!

Read Aisha's adventure next!

Aisha and her friends Mei and Quinn have an amazing secret: they can transform into powerful dragons. Together, they are the Treasure Dragon Girls, and they help keep a realm called the Magic Forest safe from harm.

The evil Shadow Sprites have stolen the Magic Mirror, determined to cause chaos among the forest's animals. Aisha must harness the power of sapphires to rescue the mirror, and return it to its rightful home in the Magic Forest's secret vault.

THE TREASURE DRAGONS

DRAGON GIRLS

We are Dragon Girls, hear us ROAR!

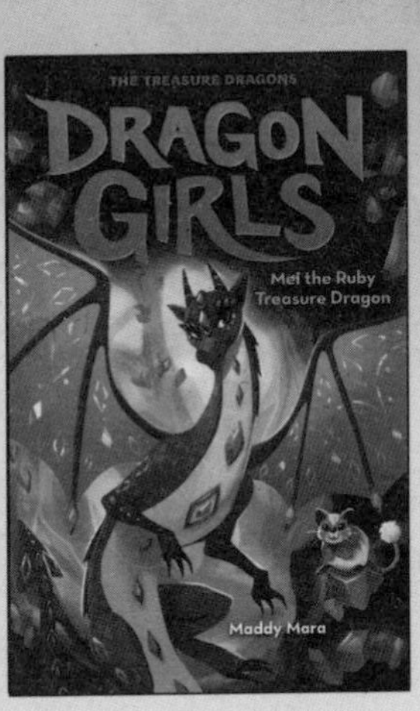

Read all three clawsome Treasure Dragon adventures!

ABOUT THE AUTHORS

Maddy Mara is the pen name of Australian creative duo Hilary Rogers and Meredith Badger. Hilary and Meredith have been collaborating on books for children for nearly two decades.

Hilary is an author and former publishing director, who has created several series that have sold into the millions. Meredith is the author of countless books for kids and young adults, and also teaches English as a foreign language to children.

The Dragon Girls is their first time co-writing under the name Maddy Mara, the melding of their respective daughters' names.